WALT DISNEY PRODUCTIONS
presents

Sir Goofy
and the Dragon

Random House 🏠 **New York**

Book Club Edition

First American Edition. Copyright © 1983 by The Walt Disney Company. All rights reserved under International and Pan-American Copyright Conventions. Published in the United States by Random House, Inc., New York, and simultaneously in Canada by Random House of Canada Limited, Toronto. Originally published in Denmark as SIR FEDTMULE OG DRAGEN by Gutenberghus Grupen, Copenhagen. ISBN: 0-394-86321-6 Manufactured in the United States of America
    890   B C D E F G H I J K

One day Mickey Mouse's nephews
were visiting Goofy.

They saw a shining sword hanging over
the fireplace.

"That's some sword, Goofy!" said Morty.

"Where did you get it?" asked Ferdy.

"This old sword?" said Goofy.
He took it down from the wall.
"Why, this sword came down to me from
the olden days," he said. "It belonged to
my great-great-grandfather Goofy."

Goofy swished the sword over his head.
"Didn't you ever hear of Sir Goofylad
of King Mickey's court?" asked Goofy.
"No," said the boys.

So Goofy told them
this tale.

Long ago in the olden days,
King Mickey ruled the land from
a great stone castle.

With him lived a band of brave knights.
They helped him keep peace in the land.

The knights practiced fighting with swords.
They went hunting with falcons.
Sometimes they rode at each other in
make-believe battles called tournaments.

The knights needed lots of weapons.
They needed metal suits of armor.
Great-great-grandfather Goofy made all
these things at his smithy.

One day some farmers came to the castle.

"Your Majesty," they said to King Mickey.
"A huge dragon has come to live in a cave
near us. He breathes smoke and fire.
He roars so loud that our houses shake!
We are afraid for our lives."

King Mickey turned to his knights.
"Go find this dragon," he said.
"You can't miss him. He roars a lot.
He breathes fire. Deal with him!"
And King Mickey went up on a tower
to watch.

The knights hurried out to the smithy.

They asked Goofy to sharpen their swords.

Goofy built up his fire and got right to work.

Next Goofy mended the suits of armor
and made sure they fit.

He got all the knights ready for battle.

Then out from
the castle rode
the brave knights.

The knights drew near to
the dragon.

They heard his roaring and
they saw his smoke.

They were scared stiff!

"Those flames will melt
our armor," said the knights.
"Let's get out of here!"

So back to the castle rode all the knights.
The farmers watched them along the way.
"That dragon is terribly dangerous," said
the knights. "We barely escaped!"

"Sorry, Your Majesty," said the knights to King Mickey.

Each had an excuse for not hunting the dragon again.

"Humph!" said King Mickey. "Some knights YOU are!"

So King Mickey had to think again.

"How can I rid this land of the dragon?"
he said. "I know. I'll offer a reward!"

So he posted a sign on the castle gate.

"Whoo-ee!" said Goofy when he read the sign.
"That's some reward! I think I'll try for it!"

REWARD

One knighthood
and
half the kingdom
to whoever
frees this land
of the dragon!
King
Mickey

Goofy went back to the smithy.
He looked through a pile of old armor.
He searched through a heap of old swords.

Goofy found
arm guards and
leg guards.

He found
a breastplate
for his chest.

He even found
feathers for a plume
on a helmet!

Goofy had no horse to ride.
He had only his faithful donkey, Sancho.
Well, Sancho would have to do!

So Goofy rode away on Sancho.

Soon he met a farmer.

"Which way to the dragon's cave?" asked Goofy.

The farmer just pointed a shaking finger.

Off went Goofy
and Sancho at
top speed!

Soon a huge roar shook the countryside.
Sancho did not like the sound of that.
He dug in his heels.
Over his head went Goofy!

Goofy rolled
down the hill.
Sancho ran
for home.

Goofy came to a stop by the dragon's cave.
"AROOO!" roared
the dragon.
He rushed outside.

"Oh, ouch!" groaned Goofy.
"I think I'm too sore to fight."
"Fight?" moaned the dragon.
"I don't want to fight! I just
want someone...

...to fix my sore paw!"

"Sore paw, eh?" Goofy
said. "Well, shut off
the smoke and I'll see
what I can do."

The dragon held his breath.
Goofy pulled a big thorn
from his paw.

"Gee, thanks!"
said the dragon.
"What a relief!"

"You know, it's hard to live
alone," said the dragon. "Could
I come live with you?"
"Why not?" said Goofy.

So Goofy and the dragon headed back
to the castle.

Everyone ran in terror at the sight
of the dragon.

Scared knights brought the news
to King Mickey.
  "The dragon is coming!"

"Man the walls!" cried King Mickey.

The knights raced
to their posts on
the castle walls.
They quickly aimed
their crossbows at
the dragon.
No one saw Goofy
on the dragon's back.
A voice called out,
"Ready, aim..."

"Stop!" cried Goofy.
"Don't shoot! It's me,
Goofy, and a friend.
Hold your fire!"

King Mickey went down to the castle gate.
"Welcome home, Goofy the Dragon Tamer!"
cried the king.

"Meet my new friend, the dragon," said Goofy to King Mickey. "He's going to live with me. He won't cause any more trouble."

"Then you have won the reward," said King Mickey.

King Mickey tapped
Goofy with a sword
and made him a knight.
"Arise, Sir Goofylad!"
said the king.

"Now half my kingdom is yours,"
said the king. "What would you like?"
"Just my old smithy," said Goofy.

Goofy and the dragon made a great team
at the smithy.

The dragon kept the fire hot all day.

Sir Goofylad turned
out the finest weapons
and armor in the land.

"So that's the story of Sir Goofylad
and the dragon," finished Goofy. "And this
is the sword that King Mickey tapped
Goofylad with. It was a royal gift."

"Wow!" said Mickey's nephews. "That's
some story. Did it really happen?"

"That's what they tell me," said Goofy.
And he smiled.